BLACKY THE CROW

BY

THORNTON W. BURGESS

With Illustrations by
HARRISON CADY

G R O S S E T & D U N L A P
Publishers   New York

Printed by arrangement with Little, Brown, and Company

CONTENTS

CONTENTS

ILLUSTRATIONS

BLACKY THE CROW

CHAPTER I

BLACKY THE CROW MAKES A DISCOVERY

BLACKY THE CROW is always watching for things not intended for his sharp eyes. The result is that he gets into no end of trouble which he could avoid. In this respect he is just like his cousin, Sammy Jay. Between them they see a great deal with which they have no business and which it would be better for them not to see.

Now Blacky the Crow finds it no easy matter to pick up a living when snow covers the Green Meadows and the Green Forest, and ice binds the Big River and the Smiling Pool. He has to use his sharp eyes for all they are worth in order to find enough to fill his stomach, and he will eat anything in the way of food that he can swallow. Often he travels long distances looking for food, but at night he always comes back to the same place in the Green Forest, to sleep in company with others of his family.

Blacky dearly loves company, particularly at night, and about the time jolly, round, red Mr. Sun is beginning to think about his bed behind the Purple Hills, you will find Blacky heading for a certain part of the Green Forest where he knows he will have neighbors of his own kind. Peter Rabbit says that it is because Blacky's conscience troubles him so that he does n't dare sleep alone, but Happy Jack Squirrel says that Blacky has n't any conscience. You can believe just which you please, though I suspect that neither of them really knows.

As I have said, Blacky is quite a traveler at this time of year, and sometimes his search for food takes him to out-of-the-way places. One day toward the very last of winter, the notion entered his black head that he would have a look in a certain lonesome corner of the Green Forest where once upon a time Redtail the Hawk had lived. Blacky knew well enough that

Redtail was n't there now; he had gone south in the fall and would n't be back until he was sure that Mistress Spring had arrived on the Green Meadows and in the Green Forest.

Like the black imp he is, Blacky flew over the tree-tops, his sharp eyes watching for something interesting below. Presently he saw ahead of him the old nest of Redtail. He knew all about that nest. He had visited it before when Redtail was away. Still it might be worth another visit. You never can tell what you may find in old houses. Now, of course, Blacky knew perfectly well that Redtail was miles and miles, hundreds of miles away, and so there was nothing to fear from him. But Blacky learned ever so long ago that there is nothing like making sure that there is no danger. So, instead of flying straight to that old nest, he first flew over the tree so that he could look down into it.

Right away he saw something that made him gasp and blink his eyes. It was quite large and white, and it looked — it looked very much indeed like an egg! Do you wonder that Blacky gasped and blinked? Here was snow on the ground, and Rough Brother North Wind and Jack Frost had given no hint that they were even thinking of going back to the Far North. The idea of any one laying an egg at this time of year! Blacky flew over to a tall pine-tree to think it over.

"Must be it was a little lump of snow," thought he. "Yet if ever I saw an egg, that looked like one. Jumping grasshoppers, how good an egg would taste right now!" You know Blacky has a weakness for eggs. The more he thought about it, the hungrier he grew. Several times he almost made up his mind to fly straight over there and make sure, but he didn't quite dare. If it were an egg, it must belong to somebody, and perhaps it would be best to find out who. Suddenly Blacky shook himself. "I must be dreaming," said he. "There couldn't, there just couldn't be an egg at this time of year, or in that old tumble-down nest! I'll just fly away and forget it."

So he flew away, but he could n't forget it. He kept thinking of it all day, and when he went to sleep that night he made up his mind to have another look at that old nest.

CHAPTER II

BLACKY MAKES SURE

"As true as ever I've cawed a caw
That was a new-laid egg I saw."

"WHAT are you talking about?" demanded Sammy Jay, coming up just in time to hear the last part of what Blacky the Crow was mumbling to himself.

"Oh nothing, Cousin, nothing at all," replied Blacky. "I was just talking foolishness to myself."

Sammy looked at him sharply. "You aren't feeling sick, are you, Cousin Blacky?" he asked. "Must be something the matter with you when you begin talking about new-laid eggs, when everything's covered with snow and ice.

Foolishness is no name for it. Whoever heard of such a thing as a new-laid egg this time of year?"

"Nobody, I guess," replied Blacky. "I told you I was just talking foolishness. You see, I'm so hungry that I just got to thinking what I'd have if I could have anything I wanted. That made me think of eggs, and I tried to think just how I would feel if I should suddenly see a great big egg right in front of me. I guess I must have said something about it."

"I guess you must have. It isn't egg time yet, and it won't be for a long time. Take my advice and just forget about impossible things. I'm going over to Farmer Brown's corncrib. Corn may not be as good as eggs, but it is very good and very filling. Better come along," said Sammy.

"Not this morning, thank you. Some other time, perhaps," replied Blacky.

He watched Sammy disappear through the trees. Then he flew to the top of the tallest pine-tree to make sure that no one was about. When he was quite sure that no one was watching him, he spread his wings and headed for the most lonesome corner of the Green Forest.

"I'm foolish. I know I'm foolish," he muttered. "But I've just got to have another look in that old nest of Redtail the Hawk. I just can't get it out of my head that that was an egg, a great, big, white egg, that I saw there yesterday. It won't do any harm to have another look, anyway."

Straight toward the tree in which was the great tumble-down nest of Redtail the Hawk he flew, and as he drew near, he flew high, for Blacky is too shrewd and smart to take any chances. Not that he thought that there could be any danger there; but you never can tell, and it is always the part of wisdom to be on the safe side. As he passed over the top of the tree, he looked down eagerly. Just imagine how he felt when instead of one, he saw *two* white things in

the old nest, — two white things
that looked for all the world like
eggs! The day before there had
been but one; now there were *two*.
That settled it in Blacky's mind;
they were eggs! They couldn't
be anything else.

Blacky kept right on flying.
Somehow he didn't dare stop just
then. He was too much excited
by what he had discovered to think
clearly. He had got to have time
to get his wits together. Whoever
had laid those eggs was big and
strong. He felt sure of that. It
must be some one a great deal
bigger than himself, and he was
of no mind to get into trouble, even
for a dinner of fresh eggs. He
must first find out whose they were;

then he would know better what
to do. He felt sure that no one
else knew about them, and he knew
that they could n't run away. So
he kept right on flying until he
reached a certain tall pine-tree
where he could sit and think without being disturbed.

"Eggs!" he muttered. "Real
eggs! Now who under the sun
can have moved into Redtail's old
house? And what can they mean
by laying eggs before Mistress
Spring has even sent word that she
has started? It's too much for
me. It certainly is too much for
me."

CHAPTER III

Two big white eggs in a tumble-down nest, and snow and ice every-where! Did ever anybody hear of such a thing before?

"Wouldn't believe it, if I hadn't seen it with my own eyes," muttered Blacky the Crow. "Have to believe them. If I can't believe them, it's of no use to try to believe anything in this world. As sure as I sit here, that old nest has two eggs in it. Whoever laid them must be crazy to start housekeeping at this time of year. I must find out whose eggs they are and then — "

Blacky did n't finish, but there was a hungry look in his eyes that would have told any who saw it, had there been any to see it, that he had a use for those eggs. But there was none to see it, and he took the greatest care that there should be none to see him when he once again started for a certain lonesome corner of the Green Forest.

"First I'll make sure that the eggs are still there," thought he, and flew high above the tree tops, so that as he passed over the tree in which was the old nest of Red-tail the Hawk, he might look down into it. To have seen him, you

would never have guessed that he
was looking for anything in particular. He seemed to be just flying over on his way to some distant
place. If the eggs were still there,
he meant to come back and hide
in the top of a near-by pine-tree
to watch until he was sure that he
might safely steal those eggs, or
to find out whose they were.

Blacky's heart beat fast with
excitement as he drew near that
old tumble-down nest. Would
those two big white eggs be there?
Perhaps there would be three!
The very thought made him flap
his wings a little faster. A few
more wing strokes and he would
be right over the tree. How he
did hope to see those eggs! He

could almost see into the nest now. One stroke! Two strokes! Three strokes! Blacky bit his tongue to keep from giving a sharp caw of disappointment and surprise.

There were no eggs to be seen. No, Sir, there wasn't a sign of eggs in that old nest. There wasn't because — why, do you think? There wasn't because Blacky looked straight down on a great mass of feathers which quite covered them from sight, and he didn't have to look twice to know that that great mass of feathers was really a great bird, the bird to whom those eggs belonged.

Blacky didn't turn to come back as he had planned. He kept right on, just as if he hadn't seen anything, and as he flew he shivered a little. He shivered at the thought of what might have happened to him if he had tried to steal those eggs the day before and had been caught doing it.

"I'm thankful I knew enough to leave them alone," said he. "Funny I never once guessed whose eggs they are. I might have known that no one but Hooty the Horned Owl would think of nesting at this time of year. And that was Mrs. Hooty I saw on the nest just now. My, but she's big! She's bigger than Hooty himself! Yes, Sir, it's a lucky thing I didn't try to get those eggs yesterday. Probably both Hooty and Mrs. Hooty were sitting close by, only they were sitting so still that I thought they were parts of the tree they were in. Blacky, Blacky, the sooner you forget those eggs the better."

> Some things are best forgotten
> As soon as they are learned.
> Who never plays with fire
> Will surely not get burned."

CHAPTER IV

Now when Blacky the Crow discovered that the eggs in the old tumble-down nest of Redtail the Hawk in a lonesome corner of the Green Forest belonged to Hooty the Owl, he straightway made the best of resolutions; he would simply forget all about those eggs. He would forget that he ever had seen them, and he would stay away from that corner of the Green Forest. That was a very wise resolution. Of all the people who live in the Green Forest, none is fiercer or more savage than Hooty the Owl, unless it is Mrs. Hooty. She is bigger than Hooty and certainly quite as much to be feared by the little people.

All this Blacky knows. No one knows it better. And Blacky is not one to poke his head into trouble with his eyes open. So he very wisely resolved to forget all about those eggs. Now it is one thing to make a resolution and quite another thing to live up to it, as you all know. It was easy enough to say that he would forget, but not at all easy to forget. It would have been different if it had been spring or early summer, when there were plenty of other eggs to be had by any one smart enough to find them and steal them. But now, when it was still winter (such an unheard-of time for any one to have eggs!), and it was hard work to find enough to keep a hungry Crow's stomach filled, the thought of those eggs *would* keep popping into his head. He just *couldn't* seem to forget them. After a little, he didn't try.

Now Blacky the Crow is very, very cunning. He is one of the smartest of all the little people who fly. No one can get into more mischief and still keep out of trouble than can Blacky the Crow. That is because he uses the wits in that black head of his. In fact, some people are unkind enough to say that he spends all his spare time in planning mischief. The more he thought of those eggs, the more he wanted them, and it wasn't long before he began to try to plan some way to get them without risking his own precious skin.

"I can't do it alone," thought he, "and yet if I take any one into my secret, I'll have to share those eggs. That won't do at all, because I want them myself. I found them, and I ought to have them." He quite forgot or overlooked the fact that those eggs really belonged to Hooty and Mrs. Hooty and to no one else. "Now let me see, what can I do?"

He thought and he thought and he thought and he thought, and little by little a plan worked out in his little black head. Then he chuckled. He chuckled right out loud, then hurriedly looked around to see if any one had heard him. No one had, so he chuckled again. He cocked his head on one side and half closed his eyes. as if that plan was something he could see and he was looking at it very hard. Then he cocked his head on the other side and did the same thing.

"It's all right," said he at last. "It'll give my relatives a lot of fun, and of course they will be very grateful to me for that. It won't hurt Hooty or Mrs. Hooty a bit, but it will make them very angry. They have very short tempers, and people with short tempers usually forget everything else when they are angry. We'll pay them a visit while the sun is bright, because then perhaps they cannot see well enough to catch us, and we'll tease them until they lose their tempers and forget all about keeping guard over those eggs. Then I'll slip in and get one and perhaps both of them. Without knowing that they are doing anything of the kind, my friends and relatives will help me to get a good meal. My, how good those eggs will taste!"

It was a very clever and cunning plan, for Blacky is a very clever and cunning rascal, but of course it didn't deserve success because nothing that means needless worry and trouble for others deserves to succeed.

CHAPTER V

BLACKY CALLS HIS FRIENDS

When Blacky cries " Caw, caw, caw, caw ! "
As if he 'd dislocate his jaw,
His relatives all hasten where
He waits them with a crafty air.

THEY know that there is mischief afoot, and the Crow family is always ready for mischief. So on this particular morning when they heard Blacky cawing at the top of his lungs from the tallest pine-tree in the Green Forest, they hastened over there as fast as they could fly, calling to each other excitedly and sure that they were going to have a good time of some kind.

Blacky chuckled as he saw them

coming. "Come on! Come on!
Caw, caw, caw! Hurry up and
flap your wings faster. I know
where Hooty the Owl is, and
we'll have no end of fun with
him," he cried.

"Caw, caw, caw, caw, caw, caw!"
shouted all his relatives in great
glee. "Where is he? Lead us to
him. We'll drive him out of the
Green Forest!"

So Blacky led the way over to
the most lonesome corner of the
Green Forest, straight to the tree
in which Hooty the Owl was comfortably sleeping. Blacky had
taken pains to slip over early
that morning and make sure just
where he was. He had discovered
Hooty fast asleep, and he knew

that he would remain right where he was until dark. You know Hooty's eyes are not meant for much use in bright light, and the brighter the light, the more uncomfortable his eyes feel. Blacky knows this, too, and he had chosen the very brightest part of the morning to call his relatives over to torment poor Hooty. Jolly, round, bright Mr. Sun was shining his very brightest, and the white snow on the ground made it seem brighter still. Even Blacky had to blink, and he knew that poor Hooty would find it harder still.

But one thing Blacky was very careful not to even hint of, and that was that Mrs. Hooty was

right close at hand. Mrs. Hooty
is bigger and even more fierce
than Hooty, and Blacky did n't
want to frighten any of the more
timid of his relatives. What he
hoped down deep in his crafty
heart was that when they got to
teasing and tormenting Hooty and
making the great racket which he
knew they would, Mrs. Hooty
would lose her temper and fly
over to join Hooty in trying to
drive away the black tormentors.
Then Blacky would slip over to the
nest which she had left unguarded
and steal one and perhaps both of
the eggs he knew were there.

When they reached the tree
where Hooty was, he was blinking
his great yellow eyes and had fluffed

out all his feathers, which is a
way he has when he is angry, to
make himself look twice as big as
he really is. Of course, he had
heard the noisy crew coming, and
he knew well enough what to ex-
pect. As soon as they saw him,
they began to scream as loud as
ever they could and to call him
all manner of names. The bold-
est of them would dart at him
as if to pull out a mouthful of
feathers, but took the greatest
care not to get too near. You
see, the way Hooty hissed and
snapped his great bill was very
threatening, and they knew that
if once he got hold of one of them
with those big cruel claws of his,
that would be the end.

So they were content to simply scold and scream at him and fly around him, just out of reach, and make him generally uncomfortable, and they were so busy doing this that no one noticed that Blacky was not joining in the fun, and no one paid any attention to the old tumble-down nest of Redtail the Hawk only a few trees distant. So far Blacky's plans were working out just as he had hoped,

CHAPTER VI

HOOTY THE OWL DOESN'T STAY STILL

Now what's the good of being smart
When others do not do their part?

IF Blacky the Crow didn't say
this to himself, he thought it. He
knew that he had made a very
cunning plan to get the eggs of
Hooty the Owl, a plan so shrewd
and cunning that no one else in
the Green Forest or on the Green
Meadows would have thought of it.
There was only one weakness in
it, and that was that it depended
for success on having Hooty the
Owl do as he usually did when
tormented by a crowd of noisy

Crows, — stay where he was until they got tired and flew away.

Now Blacky sometimes makes a mistake that smart people are very apt to make; he thinks that because he is so smart, other people are stupid. That is where he proves that smart as he is, he isn't as smart as he thinks he is. He always thought of Hooty the Owl as stupid. That is, he always thought of him that way in daytime. At night, when he was waked out of a sound sleep by the fierce hunting cry of Hooty, he wasn't so sure about Hooty being stupid, and he always took care to sit perfectly still in the darkness, lest Hooty's great ears should hear him and

Hooty's great eyes, made for seeing in the dark, should find him. No, in the night Blacky was not at all sure that Hooty was stupid.

But in the daytime he was sure. You see, he quite forgot the fact that the brightness of day is to Hooty what the blackness of night is to him. So, because Hooty would simply sit still and hiss and snap his bill, instead of trying to catch his tormentors or flying away, Blacky called him stupid. He felt sure that Hooty would stay right where he was now, and he hoped that Mrs. Hooty would lose her temper and leave the nest where she was sitting on those two eggs and join

Hooty to help him try to drive away that noisy crew.

But Hooty isn't stupid. Not a bit of it. The minute he found out that Blacky and his friends had discovered him, he thought of Mrs. Hooty and the two precious eggs in the old nest of Redtail the Hawk close by.

"Mrs. Hooty mustn't be disturbed," thought he. " That will never do at all. I must lead these black rascals away where they won't discover Mrs. Hooty. I certainly must."

So he spread his broad wings and blundered away among the trees a little way. He didn't fly far because the instant he started to fly that whole noisy crew

with the exception of Blacky were
after him. Because he couldn't
use his claws or bill while flying,
they grew bold enough to pull
a few feathers out of his back.
So he flew only a little way to
a thick hemlock-tree, where it
wasn't easy for the Crows to
get at him, and where the light
didn't hurt his eyes so much.
There he rested a few minutes
and then did the same thing over
again. He meant to lead those
bothersome Crows into the darkest
part of the Green Forest and
there—well, he could see better
there, and it might be that one
of them would be careless enough
to come within reach. No, Hooty
wasn't stupid. Certainly not.

Blacky awoke to that fact as he sat in the top of a tall pine-tree silently watching. He could see Mrs. Hooty on the nest, and as the noise of Hooty's tormentors sounded from farther and farther away, she settled herself more comfortably and closed her eyes. Blacky could imagine that she was smiling to herself. It was clear that she had no intention of going to help Hooty. His splendid plan had failed just because stupid Hooty, who was n't stupid at all, had flown away when he ought to have sat still. It was very provoking.

CHAPTER VII

BLACKY TRIES ANOTHER PLAN

When one plan fails, just try another;
Declare you'll win some way or other.

PEOPLE who succeed are those who do not give up because they fail the first time they try. They are the ones who, as soon as one plan fails, get busy right away and think of another plan and try that. If the thing they are trying to do is a good thing, sooner or later they succeed. If they are trying to do a wrong thing, very likely all their plans fail, as they should.

Now Blacky the Crow knows all about the value of trying and

trying. He is n't easily discouraged. Sometimes it is a pity that he is n't, because he plans so much mischief. But the fact remains that he is n't, and he tries and tries until he cannot think of another plan and just *has* to give up. When he invited all his relatives to join him in tormenting Hooty the Owl, he thought he had a plan that just could n't fail. He felt sure that Mrs. Hooty would leave her nest and help Hooty try to drive away his tormentors. But Mrs. Hooty did n't do anything of the kind, because Hooty was smart enough and thoughtful enough to lead his tormentors away from the nest into the darkest part of the Green

Forest where their noise would n't
bother Mrs. Hooty. So she just
settled herself more comfortably
than ever on those eggs which
Blacky had hoped she would give
him a chance to steal, and his fine
plan was quite upset.

Not one of his relatives had
noticed that nest. They had been
too busy teasing Hooty. This was
just as Blacky had hoped. He
did n't want them to know about
that nest because he was selfish
and wanted to get those eggs just
for himself alone. But now he
knew that the only way he could
get Mrs. Hooty off of them would
be by teasing her so that she
would lose her temper and try to
catch some of her tormentors. If

she did that, there would be a
chance that he might slip in and
get at least one of those eggs.
He would try it.

For a few minutes he listened
to the noise of his relatives growing fainter and fainter, as Hooty
led them farther and farther into
the Green Forest.   Then he opened
his mouth.

"Caw, caw, caw, caw!" he
screamed.   "Caw, caw, caw, caw!
Come back, everybody!   Here is
Mrs. Hooty on her nest!   Caw,
caw, caw, caw!"

Now as soon as they heard that,
all Blacky's relatives stopped chas-
ing and tormenting Hooty and
started back as fast as they could
fly.   They did n't like the dark

part of the Green Forest into
which Hooty was leading them.
Besides, they wanted to see that
nest. So back they came, cawing
at the top of their lungs, for
they were very much excited.
Some of them never had seen a nest
of Hooty's. And anyway, it would
be just as much fun to tease Mrs.
Hooty as it was to tease Hooty.

"Where is the nest?" they
screamed, as they came back to
where Blacky was cawing and pre-
tending to be very much excited.

"Why," exclaimed one, "that
is the old nest of Redtail the
Hawk. I know all about that
nest." And he looked at Blacky
as if he thought Blacky was play-
ing a joke on them.

"It was Redtail's, but it is Hooty's now. If you don't believe me, just look in it," retorted Blacky.

At once they all began to fly over the top of the tree where they could look down into the nest and there, sure enough, was Mrs. Hooty, her great, round, yellow eyes glaring up at them angrily. Such a racket! Right away Hooty was forgotten, and the whole crowd at once began to torment Mrs. Hooty. Only Blacky sat watchful and silent, waiting for Mrs. Hooty to lose her temper and try to catch one of her tormentors. He had hope, a great hope, that he would get one of those eggs.

CHAPTER VIII

HOOTY COMES TO MRS. HOOTY'S AID

No one can live just for self alone. A lot of people think they can, but they are very much mistaken. They are making one of the greatest mistakes in the world. Every teeny, weeny act, no matter what it is, affects somebody else. That is one of Old Mother Nature's great laws. And it is just as true among the little people of the Green Forest and the Green Meadows as with boys and girls and grown people. It is Old Mother Nature's way of making each of us responsible for the good

of all and of teaching us that always
we should help each other.

As you know, when Blacky the
Crow called all his relatives over
to the nest where Mrs. Hooty was
sitting on her eggs, they at once
stopped tormenting Hooty and left
him alone in a thick hemlock-tree
in the darkest part of the Green
Forest. Of course Hooty was very,
very glad to be left in peace, and
he might have spent the rest of
the day there sleeping in comfort.
But he didn't. No, Sir, he didn't.
At first he gave a great sigh of
relief and settled himself as if he
meant to stay. He listened to the
voices of those noisy Crows growing
fainter and fainter and was glad.
But it was only for a few minutes.

Presently those voices stopped growing fainter. They grew more ex-
cited-sounding than ever, and they
came right from one place. Hooty
knew then that his tormentors had
found the nest where Mrs. Hooty
was, and that they were tormenting
her just as they had tormented him.

He snapped his bill angrily and
then more angrily.

"I guess Mrs. Hooty is quite
able to take care of herself," he
grumbled, "but she ought not to
be disturbed while she is sitting on
those eggs. I hate to go back
there in that bright sunshine. It
hurts my eyes, and I don't like it,
but I guess I'll have to go back
there. Mrs. Hooty needs my help.
I'd rather stay here, but —"

He didn't finish. Instead, he spread his broad wings and flew back towards the nest and Mrs. Hooty. His great wings made no noise, for they are made so that he can fly without making a sound. "If I once get hold of one of those Crows!" he muttered to himself. "If I once get hold of one of those Crows, I'll — " He didn't say what he would do, but if you had been near enough to hear the snap of his bill, you could have guessed the rest.

All this time the Crows were having what they called fun with Mrs. Hooty. Nothing is true fun which makes others uncomfortable, but somehow a great many people seem to forget this. So, while

Blacky sat watching, his relatives
made a tremendous racket around
Mrs. Hooty, and the more angry
she grew, the more they screamed
and called her names and darted
down almost in her face, as they
pretended that they were going
to fight her. They were so busy
doing this, and Blacky was so busy
watching them, hoping that Mrs.
Hooty would leave her nest and
give him a chance to steal the eggs
he knew were under her, that no
one gave Hooty a thought.

All of a sudden he was there,
right in the tree close to the nest!
No one had heard a sound, but
there he was, and in the claws of
one foot he held the tail feathers
of one of Blacky's relatives. It

ALL OF A SUDDEN HE WAS THERE, RIGHT IN
THE TREE CLOSE TO THE NEST!

was lucky, very lucky indeed for
that one that the sun was in Hooty's
eyes and so he had missed his aim.
Otherwise there would have been
one less Crow.

Now it is one thing to tease one
lone Owl and quite another to tease
two together. Besides, there were
those black tail feathers floating
down to the snow-covered ground.
Quite suddenly those Crows decided
that they had had fun enough for
one day, and in spite of all Blacky
could do to stop them, away they
flew, cawing loudly and talking it
all over noisily. Blacky was the
last to go, and his heart was sor-
rowful. However could he get
those eggs?

CHAPTER IX

BLACKY THINKS OF FARMER BROWN'S BOY

"Such luck!" grumbled Blacky, as he flew over to his favorite tree to do a little thinking. "Such luck! Now all my neighbors know about the nest of Hooty the Owl, and sooner or later one of them will find out that there are eggs in it. There is one thing about it, though, and that is that if I can't get them, nobody can. That is to say, none of my relatives can. I've tried every way I can think of, and those eggs are still there. My, my, my, how I would like one of them right now!"

Then Blacky the Crow did a thing which disappointed scamps often do, — began to blame the ones he was trying to wrong because his plans had failed. To have heard him talking to himself, you would have supposed that those eggs really belonged to him and that Hooty and Mrs. Hooty had cheated him out of them. Yes, Sir, that is what you would have thought if you could have heard him muttering to himself there in the tree-top. In his disappointment over not getting those eggs, he was so sorry for himself that he actually did feel that he was the one wronged, — that Hooty and Mrs. Hooty should have let him have those eggs.

Of course, that was absolute
foolishness, but he made himself
believe it just the same. At least,
he pretended to believe it. And
the more he pretended, the angrier
he grew. This is often the way
with people who try to wrong
others. They grow angry with
the ones they have tried to wrong.
When at last Blacky had to confess to himself that he could think
of no other way to get those eggs,
he began to wonder if there was
some way to make trouble for
Hooty and Mrs. Hooty. It was
right then that he thought of
Farmer Brown's boy.

Blacky's eyes snapped. He
remembered how, once upon a
time, Farmer Brown's boy had

delighted to rob nests. Blacky
had seen him take the eggs from
the nests of Blacky's own relatives and from many other feathered people. What he did with
the eggs, Blacky had no idea.
Just now he didn't care. If
Farmer Brown's boy would just
happen to find Hooty's nest, he
would be sure to take those eggs,
and then he, Blacky, would feel
better. He would feel that he
was even with Hooty.

Right away he began to try to
think of some way to bring Farmer
Brown's boy over to the lonesome
corner of the Green Forest where
Hooty's nest was. If he could
once get him there, he felt sure
that Farmer Brown's boy would

see the nest and climb up to it, and then of course he would take the eggs. If he couldn't have those eggs himself, the next best thing would be to see some one else get them.

Dear me, dear me, such dreadful thoughts! I am afraid that Blacky's heart was as black as his coat. And the worst of it was, he seemed to get a lot of pleasure in his wicked plans. Now right down in his heart he knew that they were wicked plans, but he tried to make excuses to himself.

"Hooty the Owl is a robber," said he. "Everybody is afraid of him. He lives on other people, and so far as I know he does no good in the world. He is big and

fierce, and no one loves him. The
Green Forest would be better off
without him. If those eggs hatch,
there will be little Owls to be fed,
and they will grow up into big
fierce Owls, like their father and
mother. So if I show Farmer
Brown's boy that nest and he takes
those eggs, I will be doing a kindness to my neighbors."

So Blacky talked to himself and
tried to hush the still, small voice
down inside that tried to tell him
that what he was planning to do
was really a dreadful thing. And
all the time he watched for Farmer
Brown's boy.

CHAPTER X

FARMER BROWN'S boy had taken it into his head to visit the Green Forest. It was partly because he hadn't anything else to do, and it was partly because now that it was very near the end of winter he wanted to see how things were there and if there were any signs of the coming of spring. Blacky the Crow saw him coming, and Blacky chuckled to himself. He had watched every day for a week for just this thing. Now he would tell Farmer Brown's boy about that nest of Hooty the Owl.

He flew over to the lonesome

corner of the Green Forest where
Hooty and Mrs. Hooty had made
their home and at once began to
caw at the top of his voice and
pretend that he was terribly excited over something.

"Caw, caw, caw, caw, caw!"
shouted Blacky. At once all his
relatives within hearing hurried
over to join him. They knew
that he was tormenting Hooty,
and they wanted to join in the
fun. It was n't long before there
was a great racket going on over
in that lonesome corner of the
Green Forest.

Of course Farmer Brown's boy
heard it. He stopped and listened.
"Now I wonder what Blacky and
his friends have found this time,"

said he. "Whenever they make
a fuss like that, there is usually
something to see there. I believe
I'll go over and have a look."

So he turned in the direction
of the lonesome corner of the
Green Forest, and as he drew
near, he moved very carefully, so
as to see all that he could without frightening the Crows. He
knew that as soon as they saw
him, they would fly away, and
that might alarm the one they
were tormenting, for he knew
enough of Crow ways to know
that when they were making such
a noise as they were now making,
they were plaguing some one.

Blacky was the first to see
him because he was watching for

him.   But he did n't say anything until Farmer Brown's boy
was so near that he could n't
help but see that nest and Hooty
himself, sitting up very straight
and snapping his bill angrily at
his tormentors. Then Blacky gave
the alarm, and at once all the
Crows rose in the air and headed
for the Green Meadows, cawing
at the top of their lungs. Blacky
went with them a little way. The
first chance he got he dropped
out of the flock and silently flew
back to a place where he could
see all that might happen at the
nest of Hooty the Owl.

When Farmer Brown's boy first
caught sight of the nest and saw
the Crows darting down toward

it and acting so excited, he was puzzled.

"That's an old nest of Red-tail the Hawk," thought he. "I found that last spring. Now what can there be there to excite those Crows so?"

Then he caught sight of Hooty the Owl. "Ha, so that's it!" he exclaimed. "Those scamps have discovered Hooty and have been having no end of fun tormenting him. I wonder what he's doing there."

He no longer tried to keep out of sight, but walked right up to the foot of the tree, all the time looking up. Hooty saw him, but instead of flying away, he snapped his bill just as he had at the Crows and hissed.

"That's funny," thought Farmer Brown's boy. "If I didn't know that to be the old nest of Redtail the Hawk, and if it weren't still the tail-end of winter, I would think that was Hooty's nest."

He walked in a circle around the tree, looking up. Suddenly he gave a little start. Was that a tail sticking over the edge of the nest? He found a stick and threw it up. It struck the bottom of the nest, and out flew a great bird. It was Mrs. Hooty! Blacky the Crow chuckled.

CHAPTER XI

FARMER BROWN'S BOY IS TEMPTED

When you're tempted to do wrong
Is the time to prove you're strong.
Shut your eyes and clench each fist;
It will help you to resist.

WHEN a bird is found sitting on a nest, it is a pretty sure sign that that nest holds something worth while. It is a sign that that bird has set up housekeeping. So when Farmer Brown's boy discovered Mrs. Hooty sitting so close on the old nest of Redtail the Hawk, in the most lonesome corner of the Green Forest, he knew what it meant. Perhaps I should say that he knew what it ought to mean.

It ought to mean that there were eggs in that nest.

But it was hard for Farmer Brown's boy to believe that. Why, spring had not come yet! There was still snow, and the Smiling Pool was still covered with ice. Who ever heard of birds nesting at this time of year? Certainly not Farmer Brown's boy. And yet Hooty the Owl and Mrs. Hooty were acting for all the world as feathered folks do act when they have eggs and are afraid that something is going to happen to them. It was very puzzling.

"That nest was built by Red-tail the Hawk, and it has n't even been repaired," muttered

Farmer Brown's boy, as he stared
up at it. "If Hooty and his
wife have taken it for their home,
they are mighty poor house-
keepers. And if Mrs. Hooty has
laid eggs this time of year, she
must be crazy. I suppose the
way to find out is to climb up
there. It seems foolish, but I'm
going to do it. Those Owls
certainly act as if they are
mighty anxious about something,
and I'm going to find out what
it is."

He looked at Hooty and Mrs.
Hooty, at their hooked bills and
great claws, and decided that he
would take a stout stick along with
him. He had no desire to feel
these great claws. When he had

found a stick to suit him, he began to climb the tree. Hooty and Mrs. Hooty snapped their bills and hissed fiercely. They drew nearer. Farmer Brown's boy kept a watchful eye on them. They looked so big and fierce that he was almost tempted to give up and leave them in peace. But he just *had* to find out if there was anything in that nest, so he kept on. As he drew near it, Mrs. Hooty swooped very near to him, and the snap of her bill made an ugly sound. He held his stick ready to strike and kept on.

The nest was simply a great platform of sticks. When Farmer Brown's boy reached it, he found

that he could not get where he
could look into it, so he reached
over and felt inside. Almost at
once his fingers touched something
that made him tingle all over.
It was an egg, a great big egg!
There was no doubt about it.
It was just as hard for him to
believe as it had been for Blacky
the Crow to believe, when he first
saw those eggs. Farmer Brown's
boy's fingers closed over that
egg and took it out of the
nest. Mrs. Hooty swooped very
close, and Farmer Brown's boy
nearly dropped the egg as he
struck at her with his stick.
Then Mrs. Hooty and Hooty
seemed to lose courage and with-
drew to a tree near by, where

they snapped their bills and hissed.

Then Farmer Brown's boy looked at the prize in his hand. It was a big, dirty-white egg. His eyes shone. What a splendid prize to add to his collection of birds' eggs! It was the first egg of the Great Horned Owl, the largest of all Owls, that he ever had seen.

Once more he felt in the nest and found there was another egg there. "I'll take both of them," said he. "It's the first nest of Hooty's that I've ever found, and perhaps I'll never find another. Gee, I'm glad I came over here to find out what those Crows were making such a fuss about.

I wonder if I can get these down without breaking them."

Just at that very minute he remembered something. He remembered that he had stopped collecting eggs. He remembered that he had resolved never to take another bird's egg.

"But this is different," whispered the tempter. "This isn't like taking the eggs of the little song birds."

CHAPTER XII

A TREE–TOP BATTLE

As black is black and white is white,
So wrong is wrong and right is right.

THERE is n't any half way about it. A thing is wrong or it is right, and that is all there is to it. But most people have hard work to see this when they want very much to do a thing that the still small voice way down inside tells them is n't right. They try to compromise. To compromise is to do neither one thing nor the other but a little of both. But you can't do that with right and wrong. It is a queer thing, but a half right never is as good as a whole right, while a half wrong often, very often, is as bad as a whole wrong.

Farmer Brown's boy, up in the tree by the nest of Hooty the Owl in the lonesome corner of the Green Forest, was fighting a battle. No, he was n't fighting with Hooty or Mrs. Hooty. He was fighting a battle right inside himself. It was a battle between right and wrong. Once upon a time he had taken great delight in collecting the eggs of birds, in trying to see how many kinds he could get. Then as he had come to know the little forest and meadow people better, he had seen that taking the eggs of birds is very, very wrong, and he had stopped stealing them. He had declared that never again would he steal an egg from a bird.

But never before had he found a nest of Hooty the Owl. Those two big eggs would add ever so much to his collection. "Take 'em," said a little voice inside. "Hooty is a robber. You will be doing a kindness to the other birds by taking them."

"Don't do it," said another little voice. "Hooty may be a robber, but he has a place in the Green Forest, or Old Mother Nature never would have put him here. It is just as much stealing to take his eggs as to take the eggs of any other bird. He has just as much right to them as Jenny Wren has to hers."

"Take one and leave one," said the first voice.

"That will be just as much stealing as if you took both," said the second voice. "Besides, you will be breaking your own word. You said that you never would take another egg."

"I didn't promise anybody but myself," declared Farmer Brown's boy right out loud. At the sound of his voice, Hooty and Mrs. Hooty, sitting in the next tree, snapped their bills and hissed louder than ever.

"A promise to yourself ought to be just as good as a promise to any one else. I don't wonder

Hooty hisses at you," said the good little voice.

" Think how fine those eggs will look in your collection and how proud you will be to show them to the other fellows who never have found a nest of Hooty's," said the first little voice.

" And think how mean and small and cheap you 'll feel every time you look at them," added the good little voice. " You 'll get a lot more fun if you leave them to hatch out and then watch the little Owls grow up and learn all about their ways. Just think what a stout, brave fellow Hooty is to start housekeeping at this time of year, and how wonderful it is that Mrs. Hooty can keep

these eggs warm and when they
have hatched take care of the baby
Owls before others have even be-
gun to build their nests. Besides,
wrong is wrong and right is right,
always."

Slowly Farmer Brown's boy
reached over the edge of the nest
and put back the egg. Then he
began to climb down the tree.
When he reached the ground he
went off a little way and watched.
Almost at once Mrs. Hooty flew
to the nest and settled down on
the eggs, while Hooty mounted
guard close by.

"I'm glad I did n't take 'em,"
said Farmer Brown's boy. "Yes,
Sir, I'm glad I did n't take 'em."

As he turned back toward home,

he saw Blacky the Crow flying over the Green Forest, and little did he guess how he had upset Blacky's plans.

CHAPTER XIII

BLACKY HAS A CHANGE OF HEART

BLACKY THE CROW is n't all black. No, indeed. His coat is black, and sometimes it seems as if his heart is all black, but this is n't so. It certainly seemed as if his heart was all black when he tried so hard to make trouble for Hooty the Owl. It would seem as if only a black heart could have urged him to try so hard to steal the eggs of Hooty and Mrs. Hooty, but this was n't really so. You see, it did n't seem at all wrong to try to get those eggs. Blacky was hungry, and those eggs would have given him a good meal. He knew that Hooty wouldn't hesitate to catch him and eat him if he had the chance, and so it seemed to him perfectly right and fair to steal Hooty's eggs if he was smart enough to do so. And most of the other little people of the Green Forest and the Green Meadows would have felt the same way about it. You see, it is one of the laws of Old Mother Nature that each one must learn to look out for himself.

But when Blacky showed that nest of Hooty's to Farmer Brown's boy with the hope that Farmer Brown's boy would steal those eggs, there *was* blackness in his heart. He was doing something

then which was pure meanness.
He was just trying to make
trouble for Hooty, to get even
because Hooty had been too smart
for him. He had sat in the top
of a tall pine-tree where he could
see all that happened, and he had
chuckled wickedly as he had seen
Farmer Brown's boy climb to
Hooty's nest and take out an
egg. He felt sure that he would
take both eggs. He hoped so,
anyway.

When he saw Farmer Brown's
boy put the eggs back and climb
down the tree without any, he
had to blink his eyes to make
sure that he saw straight. He
just couldn't believe what he saw.
At first he was dreadfully dis-

appointed and angry. It looked
very much as if he weren't going
to get even with Hooty after all.
He flew over to his favorite tree
to think things over. Now sometimes it is a good thing to sit
by oneself and think things over.
It gives the little small voice
deep down inside a chance to be
heard. It was just that way with
Blacky now.

The longer he thought, the
meaner his action in calling Farmer Brown's boy looked. It was
one thing to try to steal those
eggs himself, but it was quite
another matter to try to have
them stolen by some one against
whom Hooty had no protection
whatever.

"If it had been any one but
Hooty, you would have done your
best to have kept Farmer Brown's
boy away," said the little voice
inside. Blacky hung his head.
He knew that it was true. More
than once, in fact many times,
he had warned other feathered
folks when Farmer Brown's boy
had been hunting for their nests,
and had helped to lead him away.

At last Blacky threw up his
head and chuckled, and this time
his chuckle was good to hear.
"I'm glad that Farmer Brown's
boy didn't take those eggs," said
he right out loud. "Yes, sir,
I'm glad. I'll never do such a
thing as that again. I'm ashamed
of what I did; yet I'm glad I

did it. I'm glad because I've
learned some things. I've learned
that Farmer Brown's boy isn't
as much to be feared as he used
to be. I've learned that Hooty
isn't as stupid as I thought he
was. I've learned that while it
may be all right for us people of
the Green Forest to try to out-
wit each other we ought to protect each other against common
dangers. And I've learned something I didn't know before, and
that is that Hooty the Owl is
the very first of us to set up
housekeeping. Now I think I'll
go hunt for an honest meal."
And he did.

CHAPTER XIV

BLACKY MAKES A CALL

Judge no one by his style of dress;
Your ignorance you thus confess.
Blacky the Crow.

"Caw, caw, caw, caw." There
was no need of looking to see who
that was. Peter Rabbit knew without looking. Mrs. Quack knew without looking. Just the same, both
looked up. Just alighting in the
top of a tall tree was Blacky the
Crow. "Caw, caw, caw, caw,"
he repeated, looking down at Peter
and Mrs. Quack and Mr. Quack
and the six young Quacks. "I
hope I am not interrupting any
secret gossip."

"I HOPE I AM NOT INTERRUPTING ANY SECRET
GOSSIP."

"Not at all," Peter hastened to say. "Mrs. Quack was just telling me of the troubles and dangers in bringing up a young family in the Far North. How did you know the Quacks had arrived?"

Blacky chuckled hoarsely. "I did n't," said he. "I simply thought there might be something going on I did n't know about over here in the pond of Paddy the Beaver, so I came over to find out. Mr. Quack, you and Mrs. Quack are looking very fine this fall. And those handsome young Quacks, you don't mean to tell me that they are your children!"

Mrs. Quack nodded proudly. "They are," said she.

" You don't say so!" exclaimed
Blacky, as if he were very much
surprised, when all the time he
wasn't surprised at all. "They
are a credit to their parents.
Yes, indeed, they are a credit to
their parents. Never have I seen
finer young Ducks in all my life.
How glad the hunters with terrible guns will be to see them."

Mrs. Quack shivered at that,
and Blacky saw it. He chuckled
softly. You know he dearly loves
to make others uncomfortable. "I
saw three hunters over on the
edge of the Big River early this
very morning," said he.

Mrs. Quack looked more anxious than ever. Blacky's sharp
eyes noted this.

"That is why I came over here," he added kindly. "I wanted to give you warning."

"But you didn't know the Quacks were here!" spoke up Peter.

"True enough, Peter. True enough," replied Blacky, his eyes twinkling. "But I thought they might be. I had heard a rumor that those who go south are traveling earlier than usual this fall, so I knew I might find Mr. and Mrs. Quack over here any time now. Is it true, Mrs. Quack, that we are going to have a long, hard, cold winter?"

"That is what they say up in the Far North," replied Mrs. Quack. "And it is true that Jack Frost had started down earlier than usual. That is how it happens we are here now. But about those hunters over by the Big River, do you suppose they will come over here?" There was an anxious note in Mrs. Quack's voice.

"No," replied Blacky promptly. "Farmer Brown's boy won't let them. I know. I've been watching him and he has been watching those hunters. As long as you stay here, you will be safe. What a great world this would be if all those two-legged creatures were like Farmer Brown's boy."

"Wouldn't it!" cried Peter. Then he added, "I wish they were."

"You don't wish it half as much as I do," declared Mrs. Quack.

"Yet I can remember when he used to hunt with a terrible gun and was as bad as the worst of them," said Blacky.

"What changed him?" asked Mrs. Quack, looking interested.

"Just getting really acquainted with some of the little people of the Green Forest and the Green Meadows," replied Blacky. "He found them ready to meet him more than halfway in friendship and that some of them really are his best friends."

"And now he is their best friend," spoke up Peter.

Blacky nodded. "Right, Peter," said he. "That is why the Quacks are safe here and will be as long as they stay."

CHAPTER XV

BLACKY DOES A LITTLE LOOKING ABOUT

Do not take the word of others
That things are or are not so
When there is a chance that you may
Find out for yourself and *know*.

Blacky the Crow.

BLACKY THE CROW is a shrewd
fellow. He is one of the smartest
and shrewdest of all the little
people in the Green Forest and
on the Green Meadows. Everybody knows it. And because of
this, all his neighbors have a great
deal of respect for him, despite his
mischievous ways.

Of course, Blacky had noticed
that Johnny Chuck had dug his

JOHNNY CHUCK HAD STUFFED HIMSELF UNTIL HE WAS FATTER THAN EVER BEFORE.

house deeper than usual and had
stuffed himself until he was fatter
than ever before. He had noticed
that Jerry Muskrat was making
the walls of his house thicker than
in other years, and that Paddy the
Beaver was doing the same thing
to his house. You know there is
very little that escapes the sharp
eyes of Blacky the Crow.

He had guessed what these
things meant. "They think we
are going to have a long, hard,
cold winter," muttered Blacky to
himself. "Perhaps they know,
but I want to see some signs of
it for myself. They may be only
guessing. Anybody can do that,
and one guess is as good as
another."

Then he found Mr. and Mrs. Quack, the Mallard Ducks, and their children in the pond of Paddy the Beaver and remembered that they never had come down from their home in the Far North as early in the fall as this. Mrs. Quack explained that Jack Frost had already started south, and so they had started earlier to keep well ahead of him.

"Looks as if there may be something in this idea of a long, hard, cold winter," thought Blacky, "but perhaps the Quacks are only guessing, too. I wouldn't take their word for it any more than I would the word of Johnny Chuck or Jerry Muskrat or Paddy the Beaver. I'll look about a little."

So after warning the Quacks to remain in the pond of Paddy the Beaver if they would be safe, Blacky bade them good-by and flew away. He headed straight for the Green Meadows and Farmer Brown's cornfield. A little of that yellow corn would make a good breakfast.

When he reached the cornfield, Blacky perched on top of a shock of corn, for it already had been cut and put in shocks in readiness to be carted up to Farmer Brown's barn. For a few minutes he sat there silent and motionless, but all the time his sharp eyes were making sure that no enemy was hiding behind one of those brown shocks. When he was quite certain that things were as safe as they seemed, he picked out a plump ear of corn and began to tear open the husks, so as to get at the yellow grains.

"Seems to me these husks are unusually thick," muttered Blacky, as he tore at them with his stout bill. "Don't remember ever having seen them as thick as these. Wonder if it just happens to be so on this ear."

Then, as a sudden thought popped into his black head, he left that ear and went to another. The husks of this were as thick as those on the first. He flew to another shock and found the husks there just the same. He tried a third shock with the same result.

"Huh, they are all alike," said
he.   Then he looked thoughtful
and for a few minutes sat perfectly
still like a black statue. "They
are right," said he at last. "Yes,
Sir, they are right."   Of course he
meant Johnny Chuck and Jerry
Muskrat and Paddy the Beaver
and the Quacks. "I don't know
how they know it, but they are
right; we are going to have a
long, hard, cold winter. I know
it myself now. I've found a sign.
Old Mother Nature has wrapped
this corn in extra thick husks, and
of course she has done it to protect
it.   She doesn't do things without
a reason. We are going to have
a cold winter, or my name isn't
Blacky the Crow."

CHAPTER XVI

BLACKY FINDS OTHER SIGNS

A single fact may fail to prove you either right
  or wrong;
Confirm it with another and your proof will
  then be strong.

Blacky the Crow.

AFTER his discovery that Old
Mother Nature had wrapped all the
ears of corn in extra thick husks,
Blacky had no doubt in his own
mind that Johnny Chuck and Jerry
Muskrat and Paddy the Beaver and
the Quacks were quite right in feeling that the coming winter would
be long, hard and cold.   But Blacky
long ago learned that it is n't wise or
wholly safe to depend altogether on
one thing.

"Old Mother Nature never does things by halves," thought Blacky, as he sat on the fence post on the Green Meadows, thinking over his discovery of the thick husks on the corn. "She would n't take care to protect the corn that way and not do as much for other things. There must be other signs, if I am smart enough to find them."

He lifted one black wing and began to set in order the feathers beneath it. Suddenly he made a funny little hop straight up.

"Well, I never!" he exclaimed, as he spread his wings to regain his balance. "I never did!"

"Is that so?" piped a squeaky little voice. "If you say you never did, I suppose you never did,

though I want the word of some
one else before I will believe it.
What is it you never did?"

Blacky looked down. Peeping
up at him from the brown grass
were two bright little eyes.

"Hello, Danny Meadow Mouse!"
exclaimed Blacky. "I haven't seen
you for a long time. I've looked
for you several times lately."

"I don't doubt it. I don't
doubt it at all," squeaked Danny.
"You'll never see me when you are
looking for me. That is, you won't
if I can help it. You won't if I
see you first."

Blacky chuckled. He knew what
Danny meant. When Blacky goes
looking for Danny Meadow Mouse,
it usually is in hope of having a

Meadow Mouse dinner, and he knew that Danny knew this. "I've had my breakfast," said Blacky, "and it isn't dinner time yet."

"What is it you never did?" persisted Danny, in his squeaky voice.

"That was just an exclamation," explained Blacky. "I made a discovery that surprised me so I exclaimed right out."

"What was it?" demanded Danny.

"It was that the feathers of my coat are coming in thicker than I ever knew them to before. I hadn't noticed it until I started to set them in order a minute ago." He buried his bill in the feathers of his breast. "Yes, sir," said he in a muffled voice, "they are coming in thicker than I ever knew them to before. There is a lot of down around the roots of them. I am going to have the warmest coat I've ever had."

"Well, don't think you are the only one," retorted Danny. "My fur never was so thick at this time of year as it is now, and it is the same way with Nanny Meadow Mouse and all our children. I suppose you know what it means."

"What does it mean?" asked Blacky, just as if he did n't have the least idea, although he had guessed the instant he discovered those extra feathers.

"It means we are going to have

a long, hard, cold winter, and Old
Mother Nature is preparing us for
it," replied Danny, quite as if he
knew all about it. "You'll find
that everybody who does n't go south
or sleep all winter has a thicker
coat than usual. Hello! There is
old Roughleg the Hawk! He has
come extra early this year. I
think I'll go back to warn Nanny."

Without another word Danny
disappeared in the brown grass.
Again Blacky chuckled. "More
signs," said he to himself. "More
signs. There is n't a doubt that
we are going to have a hard
winter. I wonder if I can stand
it or if I'd better go a little way
south, where it will be warmer."

CHAPTER XVII

BLACKY WATCHES A QUEER PERFORMANCE

This much to me is very clear:
A thing not understood is queer.
Blacky the Crow.

BLACKY THE CROW may be right. Again he may not be. If he is right, it will account for a lot of the queer people in the world. They are not understood, and so they are queer. At least, that is what other people say, and never once think that perhaps they are the queer ones for not understanding.

But Blacky isn't like those people who are satisfied not to understand and to think other people and things queer. He does his best to understand. He waits and watches and uses those sharp eyes of his and those quick wits of his until at last usually he does understand.

The day of his discovery of Old Mother Nature's signs that the coming winter would be long, hard and cold, Blacky paid a visit to the Big River. Long ago he discovered that many things are to be seen on or beside the Big River, things not to be seen elsewhere. So there are few days in which he does not get over there.

As he drew near the Big River, he was very watchful and careful, was Blacky, for this was the season when hunters with terrible guns were abroad, and he had discovered that they were likely to be hiding along the Big River, hoping to shoot Mr. or Mrs. Quack or some of their relatives. So he was very watchful as he drew near the Big River, for he had learned that it was dangerous to pass too near a hunter with a terrible gun. More than once he had been shot at. But he had learned by these experiences. Oh, yes, Blacky had learned. For one thing, he had learned to know a gun when he saw it. For another thing, he had learned just how far away one of these dreadful guns could be and still hurt the one it was pointed at, and to always keep just a

little farther away. Also he had
learned that a man or boy without a terrible gun is quite harmless, and he had learned that
hunters with terrible guns are
tricky and sometimes hide from
those they seek to kill, so that
in the dreadful hunting season it
is best to look sharply before ap-
proaching any place.

On this afternoon, as he drew
near the Big River, he saw a
man who seemed to be very busy
on the shore of the Big River,
at a place where wild rice and
rushes grew for some distance out
in the water, for just there it was
shallow far out from the shore.
Blacky looked sharply for a
terrible gun. But the man had

none with him and therefore was
not to be feared. Blacky boldly
drew near until he was able to
see what the man was doing.

Then Blacky's eyes stretched
their widest and he almost cawed
right out with surprise. The
man was taking yellow corn from
a bag, a handful at a time, and
throwing it out in the water.
Yes, Sir, that is what he was
doing, scattering nice yellow corn
among the rushes and wild rice
in the water!

"That's a queer performance,"
muttered Blacky, as he watched.
"What is he throwing perfectly
good corn out in the water for?
He isn't planting it, for this isn't
the planting season. Besides, it

would n't grow in the water, anyway. It is a shame to waste nice corn like that. What is he doing it for?"

Blacky flew over to a tree some distance away and alighted in the top of it to watch the queer performance. You know Blacky has very keen eyes and he can see a long distance. For a while the man continued to scatter corn and Blacky continued to wonder what he was doing it for. At last the man went away in a boat. Blacky watched him until he was out of sight. Then he spread his wings and slowly flew back and forth just above the rushes and wild rice, at the place where the man had been

scattering the corn. He could
see some of the yellow grains
on the bottom. Presently he saw
something else. " Ha ! " exclaimed
Blacky.

CHAPTER XVIII

BLACKY BECOMES VERY SUSPICIOUS

Of things you do not understand,
      Beware!
They may be wholly harmless but—
      Beware!
You'll find the older that you grow
That only things and folks you know
    Are fully to be trusted, so
      Beware!

                    Blacky the Crow.

THAT is one of Blacky's wise
sayings, and he lives up to it.
It is one reason why he has come
to be regarded by all his neighbors
as one of the smartest of all who
live in the Green Forest and on
the Green Meadow. He seldom
gets into any real trouble because
he first makes sure there is no

trouble to get into. When he dis-
covers something he does not understand, he is at once distrustful
of it.

As he watched a man scattering
yellow corn in the water from the
shore of the Big River he at once
became suspicious. He couldn't
understand why a man should
throw good corn among the rushes
and wild rice in the water, and
because he couldn't understand,
he at once began to suspect that
it was for no good purpose.
When the man left in a boat,
Blacky slowly flew over the rushes
where the man had thrown the
corn, and presently his sharp eyes
made a discovery that caused him
to exclaim right out.

What was it Blacky had discovered? Only a few feathers. No one with eyes less sharp than Blacky's would have noticed them. And few would have given them a thought if they had noticed them. But Blacky knew right away that those were feathers from a Duck. He knew that a Duck, or perhaps a flock of Ducks, had been resting or feeding in there among those rushes, and that in moving about they had left those two or three downy feathers.

"Ha!" exclaimed Blacky. "Mr. and Mrs. Quack or some of their relatives have been here. It is just the kind of a place Ducks like. Also some Ducks like corn.

If they should come back here
and find this corn, they would
have a feast, and they would be
sure to come again. That man
who scattered the corn here didn't
have a terrible gun, but that
doesn't mean that he isn't a
hunter. He may come back again,
and then he may have a terrible
gun. I'm suspicious of that man.
I am so. I believe he put that
corn here for Ducks and I don't
believe he did it out of the kindness of his heart. If it was
Farmer Brown's boy I would
know that all is well; that he
was thinking of hungry Ducks,
with few places where they can
feed in safety, as they make the
long journey from the Far North

to the Sunny South. But it
was n't Farmer Brown's boy. I
don't like the looks of it. I don't
indeed. I'll keep watch of this
place and see what happens."

All the way to his favorite
perch in a certain big hemlock-
tree in the Green Forest, Blacky
kept thinking about that corn and
the man who had seemed to be
generous with it, and the more
he thought, the more suspicious
he became. He did n't like the
looks of it at all.

"I'll warn the Quacks to keep
away from there. I'll do it the
very first thing in the morning,"
he muttered, as he prepared to
go to sleep. "If they have any
sense at all, they will stay in

the pond of Paddy the Beaver.
But if they should go over to
the Big River, they would be
almost sure to find that corn,
and if they should once find it,
they would keep going back for
more. It may be all right, but
I don't like the looks of it."

And still full of suspicions,
Blacky went to sleep.

CHAPTER XIX

BLACKY MAKES MORE DISCOVERIES

Little things you fail to see
May important prove to be.
Blacky the Crow.

ONE of the secrets of Blacky's success in life is the fact that he never fails to take note of little things. Long ago he learned that little things which in themselves seem harmless and not worth noticing may together prove the most important things in life. So, no matter how unimportant a thing may appear, Blacky examines it closely with those sharp eyes of his and remembers it.

The very first thing Blacky did,

as soon as he was awake the
morning after he discovered the
man scattering corn in the rushes
at a certain place on the edge
of the Big River, was to fly over
to the pond of Paddy the Beaver
and again warn Mr. and Mrs.
Quack to keep away from the
Big River, if they and their six
children would remain safe. Then
he got some breakfast. He ate it
in a hurry and flew straight over
to the Big River to the place
where he had seen that yellow
corn scattered.

Blacky was n't wholly surprised
to find Dusky the Black Duck,
own cousin to Mr. and Mrs.
Quack the Mallard Ducks, with
a number of his relatives in

among the rushes and wild rice
at the very place where that corn
had been scattered. They seemed
quite contented and in the best
of spirits. Blacky guessed why.
Not a single grain of that yellow
corn could Blacky see. He knew
the ways of Dusky and his relatives. He knew that they must
have come in there just at dusk
the night before and at once had
found that corn. He knew that
they would remain hiding there
until frightened out, and that then
they would spend the day in
some little pond where they would
not be likely to be disturbed or
where at least no danger could
approach them without being seen
in plenty of time. There they

would rest all day, and when the
Black Shadows came creeping out
from the Purple Hills, they would
return to that place on the Big
River to feed, for that is the
time when they like best to hunt
for their food.

Dusky looked up as Blacky
flew over him, but Blacky said
nothing, and Dusky said nothing.
But if Blacky did n't use his
tongue, he did use his eyes. He
saw just on the edge of the shore
what looked like a lot of small
bushes growing close together on
the very edge of the water. Mixed
in with them were a lot of the
brown rushes. They looked very
harmless and innocent. But Blacky
knew every foot of that shore

along the Big River, and he knew
that those bushes had n't been
there during the summer. He
knew that they had n't grown
there.

He flew directly over them.
Just back of them were a couple
of logs. Those logs had n't been
there when he passed that way a
few days before. He was sure of
it.

"Ha!" exclaimed Blacky under
his breath. "Those look to me
as if they might be very handy,
very handy indeed, for a hunter
to sit on. Sitting there behind
those bushes, he would be hidden
from any Duck who might come
in to look for nice yellow corn
scattered out there among the

rushes. It does n't look right to me. No, Sir, it does n't look right to me. I think I'll keep an eye on this place."

So Blacky came back to the Big River several times that day. The second time back he found that Dusky the Black Duck and his relatives had left. When he returned in the afternoon, he saw the same man he had seen there the afternoon before, and he was doing the same thing, — scattering yellow corn out in the rushes. And as before, he went away in a boat.

"I don't like it," muttered Blacky, shaking his black head. "I don't like it."

CHAPTER XX

BLACKY DROPS A HINT

When you see another's danger
Warn him though he be a stranger.
Blacky the Crow.

EVERY day for a week a man came in a boat to scatter corn in the rushes at a certain point along the bank of the Big River, and every day Blacky the Crow watched him and shook his black head and talked to himself and told himself that he did n't like it, and that he was sure that it was for no good purpose. Sometimes Blacky watched from a distance, and sometimes he flew right over the man. But never

once did the man have a gun
with him.

Every morning, very early,
Blacky flew over there, and every
morning he found Dusky the
Black Duck and his flock in the
rushes and wild rice at that particular place, and he knew that
they had been there all night. He
knew that they had come in
there just at dusk the night before, to feast on the yellow corn
the man had scattered there in
the afternoon.

"It is no business of mine
what those Ducks do," muttered
Blacky to himself, "but as surely
as my tail feathers are black,
something is going to happen
to some of them one of these

days. That man may be fooling
them, but he is n't fooling me.
Not a bit of it. He has n't had
a gun with him once when I
have seen him, but just the same
he is a hunter. I feel it in my
bones. He knows those silly
Ducks come in here every night
for that corn he puts out.
He knows that after they have
been here a few times and nothing has frightened them, they
will be so sure that it is a safe
place that they will not be the
least bit suspicious. Then he
will hide behind those bushes he
has placed close to the edge of the
water and wait for them with his
terrible gun. That is what he will
do, or my name is n't Blacky."

Finally Blacky decided to drop a hint to Dusky the Black Duck. So the next morning he stopped for a call. "Good morning," said he, as Dusky swam in just in front of him. "I hope you are feeling as fine as you look."

"Quack, quack," replied Dusky. "When Blacky the Crow flatters, he hopes to gain something. What is it this time?"

"Not a thing," replied Blacky. "On my honor, not a thing. There is nothing for me here, though there seems to be plenty for you and your relatives, to judge by the fact that I find you in this same place every morning. What is it?"

"Corn," replied Dusky in a low voice, as if afraid some one might overhear him. "Nice yellow corn."

"Corn!" exclaimed Blacky, as if very much astonished. "How does corn happen to be way over here in the water?"

Dusky shook his head. "Don't ask me, for I can't tell you," said he. "I have n't the least idea. All I know is that every evening when we arrive, we find it here. How it gets here, I don't know, and furthermore I don't care. It is enough for me that it is here."

"I've seen a man over here every afternoon," said Blacky. "I thought he might be a hunter."

"Did he have a terrible gun?" asked Dusky suspiciously.

"No-o," replied Blacky.

"Then he isn't a hunter," declared Dusky, looking much relieved.

"But perhaps one of these days he will have one and will wait for you to come in for your dinner," suggested Blacky. "He could hide behind these bushes, you know."

"Nonsense," retorted Dusky, tossing his head. "There hasn't been a sign of danger here since we have been here. I know you, Blacky; you are jealous because we find plenty to eat here, and you find nothing. You are trying to scare us. But I'll tell you right now, you can't scare us away from such splendid eating as we have had here. So there!"

XXI

AT LAST BLACKY IS SURE

Who for another conquers fear
Is truly brave, it is most clear.

Blacky the Crow.

IT was late in the afternoon, and Blacky the Crow was on his way to the Green Forest. As usual, he went around by the Big River to see if that man was scattering corn for the Ducks. He was n't there. No one was to be seen along the bank of the Big River.

"He has n't come to-day, or else he came early and has left," thought Blacky. And then his sharp eyes caught sight of something that made him turn aside and make straight for a certain tree, from the top of which he could see all that went on for a long distance. What was it Blacky saw? It was a boat coming down the Big River.

Blacky sat still and watched. Presently the boat turned in among the rushes, and a moment later a man stepped out on the shore. It was the same man Blacky had watched scatter corn in the rushes every day for a week. There was n't the least doubt about it, it was the same man.

"Ha, ha!" exclaimed Blacky, and nearly lost his balance in his excitement. "Ha, ha! It is just as I thought!" You see Blacky's sharp eyes had seen that the man was carrying something, and that

something was a gun, a terrible
gun. Blacky knows a terrible gun
as far as he can see it.

The hunter, for of course that
is what he was, tramped along the
shore until he reached the bushes
which Blacky had noticed close to
the water and which he knew had
not grown there. The hunter
looked out over the Big River.
Then he walked along where he
had scattered corn the day before.
Not a grain was to be seen. This
seemed to please him. Then he
went back to the bushes and sat
down on a log behind them, his
terrible gun across his knees.

"I was sure of it," muttered
Blacky. "He is going to wait
there for those Ducks to come in,

and then something dreadful will happen. What terrible creatures these hunters are ! They don't know what fairness is. No, Sir, they don't know what fairness is. He has put food there day after day, where Dusky the Black Duck and his flock would be sure to find it, and has waited until they have become so sure there is no danger that they are no longer suspicious. He knows they will feel so sure that all is safe that they will come in without looking for danger. Then he will fire that terrible gun and kill them without giving them any chance at all.

"Reddy Fox is a sly, clever hunter, but he wouldn't do a thing like that. Neither would Old Man

Coyote or anybody else who wears fur or feathers. They might hide and try to catch some one by surprise. That is all right, because each of us is supposed to be on the watch for things of that sort. Oh, dear, what's to be done? It is time I was getting home to the Green Forest. The Black Shadows will soon come creeping out from the Purple Hills, and I must be safe in my hemlock-tree by then. I would be scared to death to be out after dark. Yet those Ducks ought to be warned. Oh, dear, what shall I do?"

Blacky peered over at the Green Forest and then over toward the Purple Hills, behind which jolly, round, red Mr. Sun would go to

bed very shortly. He shivered as
he thought of the Black Shadows
that soon would come swiftly out
from the Purple Hills across the
Big River and over the Green
Meadows. With them might come
Hooty the Owl, and Hooty would n't
object in the least to a Crow dinner.
He wished he was in that hemlock-
tree that very minute.

Then Blacky looked at the hunter
with his terrible gun and thought
of what might happen, what would
be almost sure to happen, unless
those Ducks were warned. "I'll
wait a little while longer," muttered
Blacky, and tried to feel brave.
But instead he shivered.

CHAPTER XXII

BLACKY GOES HOME HAPPY

No greater happiness is won
Than through a deed for others done.
Blacky the Crow.

BLACKY sat in the top of a tree near the bank of the Big River and could n't make up his mind what to do. He wanted to get home to the big, thick hem. lock-tree in the Green Forest before dusk, for Blacky is afraid of the dark. That is, he is afraid to be out after dark.

"Go along home," said a voice inside him, "there is hardly time now for you to get there before the Black Shadows arrive.

Don't waste any more time here. What may happen to those silly Ducks is no business of yours, and there is nothing you can do, anyway. Go along home."

"Wait a few minutes," said another little voice down inside him. "Don't be a coward. You ought to warn Dusky the Black Duck and his flock that a hunter with a terrible gun is waiting for them. Is it true that it is no business of yours what happens to those Ducks? Think again, Blacky; think again. It is the duty of each one who sees a common danger to warn his neighbors. If something dreadful should happen to Dusky because you were afraid of the dark, you

never would be comfortable in
your own mind. Stay a little
while and keep watch."

Not five minutes later Blacky
saw something that made him, oh,
so glad he had kept watch. It
was a swiftly moving black line
just above the water far down
the Big River, and it was coming
up. He knew what that black
line was. He looked over at the
hunter hiding behind some bushes
close to the edge of the water.
The hunter was crouching with
his terrible gun in his hands and
was peeping over the bushes,
watching that black line. He,
too, knew what it was. It was
a flock of Ducks flying.

Blacky was all ashake again,

but this time it was n't with fear
of being caught away from home
in the dark; it was with excitement. He knew that those Ducks
had become so eager for more of
that corn, that delicious yellow
corn which every night for a week
they had found scattered in the
rushes just in front of the place
where that hunter was now hiding,
that they could n't wait for the
coming of the Black Shadows.
They were so sure there was no
danger that they were coming in
to eat without waiting for the
Black Shadows, as they usually
did. And Blacky was glad. Perhaps now he could give them
warning.

Up the middle of the Big

River, flying just above the water,
swept the flock with Dusky at its
head.   How swiftly they flew, those
nine big birds! Blacky envied
them their swift wings.   On past
the hidden hunter but far out
over the Big River they swept.
For just a minute Blacky thought
they were going on up the river
and not coming in to eat, after
all.   Then they turned toward
the other shore, swept around in
a circle and headed straight in toward that hidden hunter.   Blacky
glanced at him and saw that he
was ready to shoot.

Almost without thinking, Blacky
spread his wings and started out
from that tree.   "Caw, caw, caw,
caw, caw!" he shrieked at the top

of his lungs. "Caw, caw, caw, caw, caw!" It was his danger cry that everybody on the Green Meadows and in the Green Forest knows.

Instantly Dusky turned and began to climb up, up, up, the other Ducks following him until, as they passed over the hidden hunter, they were so high it was useless for him to shoot. He did put up his gun and aim at them, but he didn't shoot. You see, he didn't want to frighten them so that they would not return. Then the flock turned and started off in the direction from which they had come, and in a few minutes they were merely a black line disappearing far down the Big River.

Blacky headed straight for the Green Forest, chuckling as he flew. He knew that those Ducks would not return until after dark. He had saved them this time, and he was so happy he didn't even notice the Black Shadows. And the hunter stood up and shook his fist at Blacky the Crow.

CHAPTER XXIII

BLACKY CALLS FARMER BROWN'S BOY

BLACKY awoke in the best of spirits. Late the afternoon before he had saved Dusky the Black Duck and his flock from a hunter with a terrible gun. He was n't quite sure whether he was most happy in having saved those Ducks by warning them just in time, or in having spoiled the plans of that hunter. He hates a hunter with a terrible gun, does Blacky. For that matter, so do all the little people of the Green Forest and the Green Meadows.

So Blacky started out for his breakfast in high spirits. After

breakfast, he flew over to the Big
River to see if Dusky the Black
Duck was feeding in the rushes
along the shore. Dusky was n't,
and Blacky guessed that he and
his flock had been so frightened
by that warning that they had
kept away from there the night
before.

"But they'll come back after
a night or so," muttered Blacky,
as he alighted in the top of a
tree, the same tree from which he
had watched the hunter the afternoon before. "They'll come back,
and so will that hunter. If he
sees me around again, he'll try
to shoot me. I've done all I
can do. Anyway, Dusky ought
to have sense enough to be sus-

picious of this place after that warning. Hello, who is that? I do believe it is Farmer Brown's boy. I wish he would come over here. If he should find out about that hunter, perhaps he would do something to drive him away. I'll see if I can call him over here."

Blacky began to call in the way he does when he has discovered something and wants others to know about it. "Caw, caw, caaw, caaw, caw, caw, caaw!" screamed Blacky, as if greatly excited.

Now Farmer Brown's boy, having no work to do that morning, had started for a tramp over the Green Meadows, hoping to

see some of his little friends in
feathers and fur. He heard the
excited cawing of Blacky and at
once turned in that direction.

"That black rascal has found
something over on the shore of
the Big River," said Farmer
Brown's boy to himself. "I'll go
over there to see what it is.
There isn't much escapes the
sharp eyes of that black busybody.
He has led me to a lot of interesting things, one time and
another. There he is on the top
of that tree over by the Big
River."

As Farmer Brown's boy drew
near, Blacky flew down and disappeared below the bank. Farmer
Brown's boy chuckled. "What-

ever it is, it is right down there,"
he muttered.

He walked forward rapidly but
quietly, and presently he reached
the edge of the bank. Up flew
Blacky cawing wildly, and pre-
tending to be scared half to death.
Again Farmer Brown's boy
chuckled. "You're just making
believe," he declared. "You're
trying to make me believe that
I have surprised you, when all
the time you knew I was coming
and have been waiting for me.
Now, what have you found over
here?"

He looked eagerly along the
shore, and at once he saw a row
of low bushes close to the edge
of the water. He knew what it

was instantly. "A Duck blind!"
he exclaimed. "A hunter has
built a blind over here from which
to shoot Ducks. I wonder if he
has killed any yet. I hope not."

He went down to the blind,
for that is what a Duck hunter's
hiding-place is called, and looked
about. A couple of grains of
corn just inside the blind caught
his eyes, and his face darkened.
"That fellow has been baiting
Ducks," thought he. "He has
been putting out corn to get them
to come here regularly. My, how
I hate that sort of thing! It is
bad enough to hunt them fairly,
but to feed them and then kill
them — ugh! I wonder if he has
shot any yet."

He looked all about keenly, and his face cleared. He knew that if that hunter had killed any Ducks, there would be tell-tale feathers in the blind, and there were none.

CHAPTER XXIV

FARMER BROWN'S BOY DOES SOME THINKING

FARMER BROWN'S boy sat on the bank of the Big River in a brown study. That means that he was thinking very hard. Blacky the Crow sat in the top of a tall tree a short distance away and watched him. Blacky was silent now, and there was a knowing look in his shrewd little eyes. In calling Farmer Brown's boy over there, he had done all he could, and he was quite satisfied to leave the matter to Farmer Brown's boy.

"A hunter has made that blind

to shoot Black Ducks from,"
thought Farmer Brown's boy,
"and he has been baiting them
in here by scattering corn for
them. Black Ducks are about
the smartest Ducks that fly, but
if they have been coming in here
every evening and finding corn
and no sign of danger, they probably think it perfectly safe here
and come straight in without being
at all suspicious. To-night, or
some night soon, that hunter will
be waiting for them.

"I guess the law that permits
hunting Ducks is all right, but
there ought to be a law against
baiting them in. That is n't hunting. No, Sir, that is n't hunting.
If this land were my father's. I

would know what to do. I would
put up a sign saying that this
was private property and no
shooting was allowed. But it isn't
my father's land, and that hunter
has a perfect right to shoot here.
He has just as much right here
as I have. I wish I could stop
him, but I don't see how I can."

A frown puckered the freckled
face of Farmer Brown's boy.
You see, he was thinking very
hard, and when he does that he
is very apt to frown.

"I suppose," he muttered, "I
can tear down his blind. He
wouldn't know who did it. But
that wouldn't do much good; he
would build another. Besides, it
wouldn't be right. He has a

perfect right to make a blind here, and having made it, it is his and I haven't any right to touch it. I won't do a thing I haven't a right to do. That wouldn't be honest. I've got to think of some other way of saving those Ducks."

The frown on his freckled face grew deeper, and for a long time he sat without moving. Suddenly his face cleared, and he jumped to his feet. He began to chuckle. "I have it!" he exclaimed. "I'll do a little shooting myself!" Then he chuckled again and started for home. Presently he began to whistle, a way he has when he is in good spirits.

Blacky the Crow watched him

go, and Blacky was well satisfied.
He didn't know what Farmer
Brown's boy was planning to do,
but he had a feeling that he
was planning to do something,
and that all would be well.
Perhaps Blacky wouldn't have
felt so sure could he have understood what Farmer Brown's boy
had said about doing a little
shooting himself.

As it was, Blacky flew off
about his own business, quite
satisfied that now all would be
well, and he need worry no more
about those Ducks. None of the
little people of the Green Forest
and the Green Meadows knew
Farmer Brown's boy better than
did Blacky the Crow. None knew

better than he that Farmer
Brown's boy was their best friend.

"It is all right now," chuckled
Blacky. "It is all right now."
And as the cheery whistle of
Farmer Brown's boy floated back
to him on the Merry Little
Breezes, he repeated it: "It is
all right now."

CHAPTER XXV

BLACKY GETS A DREADFUL SHOCK

When friends prove false, whom may we trust?
The springs of faith are turned to dust.

Blacky the Crow.

BLACKY THE CROW was in the top
of his favorite tree over near the
Big River early this afternoon. He
did n't know what was going to
happen, but he felt in his bones
that something was, and he meant
to be on hand to see. For a long
time he sat there, seeing nothing
unusual. At last he spied a tiny
figure far away across the Green
Meadows. Even at that distance
he knew who it was; it was Farmer

Brown's boy, and he was coming toward the Big River.

"I thought as much," chuckled Blacky. "He is coming over here to drive that hunter away."

The tiny figure grew larger. It was Farmer Brown's boy beyond a doubt. Suddenly Blacky's eyes opened so wide that they looked as if they were in danger of popping out of his head. He had discovered that Farmer Brown's boy was carrying something and that that something was a gun! Yes, Sir, Farmer Brown's boy was carrying a terrible gun! If Blacky could have rubbed his eyes, he would have done so, just to make sure that there was nothing the matter with them.

"A gun!" croaked Blacky.

"Farmer Brown's boy with a terrible gun ! What does it mean ?"

Nearer came Farmer Brown's boy, and Blacky could see that terrible gun plainly now. Suddenly an idea popped into his head. "Perhaps he is going to shoot that hunter !" thought Blacky, and somehow he felt better.

Farmer Brown's boy reached the Big River at a point some distance below the blind built by the hunter. He laid his gun down on the bank and went down to the edge of the water. The rushes grew very thick there, and for a while Farmer Brown's boy was very busy among them. Blacky frcm his high perch could watch him, and as he watched, he grew more and more puzzled. It looked very much as if Farmer Brown's boy was building a blind much like that of the hunter's. At last he carried an old log down there, got his gun, and sat down just as the hunter had done in his blind the afternoon before. He was quite hidden there, excepting from a place high up like Blacky's perch.

"I — I — I do believe he is going to try to shoot those Ducks himself," gasped Blacky. "I would n't have believed it if any one had told me. No, Sir, I would n't have believed it. I — I — can't believe it now. Farmer Brown's boy hunting with a terrible gun! Yet I've got to believe my own eyes."

A noise up river caught his

attention.   It was the noise of oars
in a boat.   There was the hunter,
rowing down the Big River.   Just
as he had done the day before, he
came ashore above his blind and
walked down to it.

"This is no place for me,"
muttered Blacky. "He'll remember
that I scared those Ducks yesterday,
and as likely as not he'll try to
shoot me."

Blacky spread his black wings
and hurriedly left the tree-top,
heading for another tree farther
back on the Green Meadows where
he would be safe, but from which
he could not see as well.   There he
sat until the Black Shadows warned
him that it was high time for him to
be getting back to the Green Forest.

He had to hurry, for it was later than usual, and he was afraid to be out after dark. Just as he reached the Green Forest he heard a faint "bang, bang" from over by the Big River, and he knew that it came from the place where Farmer Brown's boy was hiding in the rushes.

"It is true," croaked Blacky. "Farmer Brown's boy has turned hunter." It was such a dreadful shock to Blacky that it was a long time before he could go to sleep.

CHAPTER XXVI

WHY THE HUNTER GOT NO DUCKS

THE hunter who had come down the Big River in a boat and landed near the place where Dusky the Black Duck and his flock had found nice yellow corn scattered in the rushes night after night saw Blacky the Crow leave the top of a certain tree as he approached.

"It is well for you that you did n't wait for me to get nearer," said the hunter. "You are smart enough to know that you can't play the same trick on me twice. You frightened those Ducks away last

night, but if you try it again,
you'll be shot as surely as your
coat is black."

Then the hunter went to his
blind which, you know, was the
hiding-place he had made of
bushes and rushes, and behind
this he sat down with his terrible
gun to wait and watch for Dusky
the Black Duck and his flock.

Now you remember that farther along the shore of the Big
River was Farmer Brown's boy,
hiding in a blind he had made
that afternoon. The hunter
couldn't see him at all. He
didn't have the least idea that
any one else was anywhere near.
" With that Crow out of the way,
I think I will get some Ducks

to-night," thought the hunter and looked at his gun to make sure that it was ready.

Over in the West, jolly, round, red Mr. Sun started to go to bed behind the Purple Hills, and the Black Shadows came creeping out. Far down the Big River the hunter saw a swiftly moving black line just above the water. "Here they come," he muttered, as he eagerly watched that black line draw nearer.

Twice those big black birds circled around over the Big River opposite where the hunter was crouching behind his blind. It was plain that Dusky, their leader, remembered Blacky's warning the night before. But this time

there was no warning. Everything appeared safe. Once more
the flock circled and then headed
straight for that place where they
hoped to find more corn. The
hunter crouched lower. They
were almost near enough for him
to shoot when "bang, bang"
went a gun a short distance
away.

Instantly Dusky and his flock
turned and on swift wings swung
off and up the river. If ever
there was a disappointed hunter,
it was the one crouching in that
blind. "Somebody else is hunting, and he spoiled my shot that
time," he muttered. "He must
have a blind farther down. Probably some other Ducks I did n'

see came in to him. I wonder
if he got them. Here's hoping
that next time those Ducks come
in here first."

He once more made himself
comfortable and settled down for
a long wait. The Black Shadows
crept out from the farther bank
of the Big River. Jolly, round
red Mr. Sun had gone to bed,
and the first little star was twinkling high overhead. It was very
still and peaceful. From out in
the middle of the Big River
sounded a low "quack"; Dusky
and his flock were swimming in
this time. Presently the hunter
could see a silver line on the
water, and then he made out
nine black spots. In a few min-

utes those Ducks would be where he could shoot them.

"Bang, bang" went that gun below him again. With a roar of wings, Dusky and his flock were in the air and away. That hunter stood up and said things, and they were not nice things. He knew that those Ducks would not come back again that night, and that once more he must go home empty-handed. But first he would find out who that other hunter was and what luck he had had, so he tramped down the shore to where that gun had seemed to be. He found the blind of Farmer Brown's boy, but there was no one there. You see, as soon as he had fired his

gun the last time, Farmer Brown's
boy had slipped out and away.
And as he tramped across the
Green Meadows toward home with
his gun, he chuckled. "He did n't
get those Ducks this time," said
Farmer Brown's boy.

CHAPTER XXVII

THE HUNTER GIVES UP

BLACKY THE CROW did n't know what to think. He could n't make himself believe that Farmer Brown's boy had really turned hunter, yet what else could he believe? Had n't he with his own eyes seen Farmer Brown's boy with a terrible gun hide in rushes along the Big River and wait for Dusky the Black Duck and his flock to come in? And had n't he with his own ears heard the "bang, bang" of that very gun?

The very first thing the next morning Blacky had hastened over to the place where Farmer Brown's boy had hidden in the rushes. With sharp eyes he looked for feathers, that would tell the tale of a Duck killed. But there were no feathers. There wasn't a thing to show that anything so dreadful had happened. Perhaps Farmer Brown's boy had missed when he shot at those Ducks. Blacky shook his head and decided to say nothing to anybody about Farmer Brown's boy and that terrible gun.

You may be sure that early in the afternoon he was perched in the top of his favorite tree over by the Big River. His heart sank, just as on the afternoon before, when he saw Farmer Brown's boy with his terrible gun trudging across

the Green Meadows to the Big
River. Instead of going to the
same hiding place he made a new
one farther down.

Then came the hunter a little
earlier than usual. Instead of
stopping at his blind, he walked
straight to the blind Farmer Brown's
boy had first made. Of course,
there was no one there. The
hunter looked both glad and disappointed. He went back to his
own blind and sat down, and while
he watched for the coming of the
Ducks, he also watched that other
blind to see if the unknown hunter
of the night before would appear.
Of course he did n't, and when at
last the hunter saw the Ducks
coming, he was sure that this

time he would get some of them.

But the same thing happened as on the night before. Just as those Ducks were almost near enough, a gun went "bang, bang," and away went the Ducks. They did n't come back again, and once more a disappointed hunter went home without any.

The next afternoon he was on hand very early. He was there before Farmer Brown's boy arrived, and when he did come, of course the hunter saw him. He walked down to where Farmer Brown's boy was hiding in the rushes. "Hello!" said he. "Are you the one who was shooting here last night and the night before?"

Farmer Brown's boy grinned. "Yes," said he.

"What luck did you have?" asked the hunter.

"Fine," replied Farmer Brown's boy.

"How many Ducks did you get?" asked the hunter.

Farmer Brown's boy grinned more broadly than before. "None," said he. "I guess I'm not a very good shot."

"Then what did you mean by saying you had fine luck?" demanded the hunter.

"Oh," replied Farmer Brown's boy, "I had the luck to see those Ducks and the fun of shooting," and he grinned again.

The hunter lost patience. He

tried to order Farmer Brown's boy
away. But the latter said he had
as much right there as the hunter
had, and the hunter knew that this
was so. Finally he gave up, and
muttering angrily, he went back to
his blind. Again the gun of Farmer
Brown's boy frightened away the
Ducks just as they were coming
in.

The next afternoon there was
no hunter nor the next, though
Farmer Brown's boy was there.
The hunter had decided that it
was a waste of time to hunt there
while Farmer Brown's boy was
about.

CHAPTER XXVIII

BLACKY HAS A TALK WITH DUSKY THE BLACK DUCK

Doubt not a friend, but to the last
Grip hard on faith and hold it fast.
Blacky the Crow.

EVERY morning Blacky the Crow visited the rushes along the shore of the Big River, hoping to find Dusky the Black Duck. He was anxious, was Blacky. He feared that Dusky or some of his flock had been killed, and he wanted to know. You see, he knew that Farmer Brown's boy had been shooting over there. At last, early one morning, he found Dusky and his flock in the rushes and wild rice. Eagerly he counted them. There were nine. Not one was missing. Blacky sighed with relief and dropped down on the shore close to where Dusky was taking a nap.

"Hello!" said Blacky.

Dusky awoke with a start. "Hello, yourself," said he.

"I've heard a terrible gun banging over here, and I was afraid you or some of your flock had been shot," said Blacky.

"We haven't lost a feather," declared Dusky. "That gun wasn't fired at us, anyway."

"Then who was it fired at?" demanded Blacky.

"I haven't the least idea," replied Dusky.

"Have you seen any other Ducks about here?" inquired Blacky.

"Not one," was Dusky's prompt reply. "If there had been any, I guess we would have known it."

"Did you know that when that terrible gun was fired there was another terrible gun right over behind those bushes?" asked Blacky.

Dusky shook his head. "No," said he, "but I learned long ago that where there is one terrible gun there is likely to be more, and so when I heard that one bang, I led my flock away from here in a hurry. We did n't want to take any chances."

"It is a lucky thing you did," replied Blacky. "There was a

hunter hiding behind those bushes
all the time. I warned you of
him once."

"That reminds me that I
haven't thanked you," said
Dusky. "I knew there was
something wrong over here, but
I didn't know what. So it was
a hunter. I guess it is a good
thing that I heeded your warning."

"I guess it is," retorted Blacky
dryly. "Do you come here in
daytime instead of night now?"

"No," replied Dusky. "We
come in after dark and spend
the night here. There is nothing
to fear from hunters after dark.
We've given up coming here until late in the evening. And

since we did that, we haven't heard a gun."

Blacky gossiped a while longer, then flew off to look for his breakfast; and as he flew his heart was light. His shrewd little eyes twinkled.

"I ought to have known Farmer Brown's boy better than even to suspect him," thought he. "I know now why he had that terrible gun. It was to frighten those Ducks away so that the hunter would not have a chance to shoot them. He wasn't shooting at anything. He just fired in the air to scare those Ducks away. I know it just as well as if I had seen him do it. I'll never doubt Farmer Brown's boy again.

And I'm glad I didn't say a word to anybody about seeing him with a terrible gun."

Blacky was right. Farmer Brown's boy had taken that way of making sure that the hunter who had first baited those Ducks with yellow corn scattered in the rushes in front of his hiding place should have no chance to kill any of them. While appearing to be an enemy, he really had been a friend of Dusky the Black Duck and his flock.

CHAPTER XXIX

BLACKY DISCOVERS AN EGG

BLACKY is fond of eggs, as you know. In this he is a great deal like other people, Farmer Brown's boy for instance. But as Blacky cannot keep hens, as Farmer Brown's boy does, he is obliged to steal eggs or else go without. If you come right down to plain, everyday truth, I suppose Blacky isn't so far wrong when he insists that he is no more of a thief than Farmer Brown's boy. Blacky says that the eggs which the hens lay belong to the hens, and that he, Blacky has just as much right to take them as Farmer Brown's boy. He quite overlooks the fact that Farmer Brown's boy feeds the biddies and takes the eggs as pay. Anyway, that is what Farmer Brown's boy says, but I do not know whether or not the biddies understand it that way.

So Blacky the Crow cannot see why he should not help himself to an egg when he gets the chance. He doesn't get the chance very often to steal eggs from the hens, because usually they lay their eggs in the henhouse, and Blacky is too suspicious to venture inside. The eggs he does get are mostly those of his neighbors in the Green Forest

and the Old Orchard. But once
in a great while some foolish hen
will make a nest outside the henhouse somewhere, and if Blacky
happens to find it the black
scamp watches every minute he
can spare from other mischief for
a chance to steal an egg.

Now Blacky knows just what
a rogue Farmer Brown's boy
thinks he is, and for this reason
Blacky is very careful about ap-
proaching Farmer Brown or any
other man until he has made
sure that he runs no risk of
being shot. Blacky knows quite
as well as any one what a gun
looks like. He also knows that
without a terrible gun, there is
little Farmer Brown or any one

else can do to him. So when he
sees Farmer Brown out in his
fields, Blacky often will fly right
over him and shout " Caw, caw,
caw, ca-a-w ! " in the most provoking way, and Farmer Brown's
boy insists that he has seen
Blacky wink when he was doing
it.

But Blacky does n't do anything of this kind around the
buildings of Farmer Brown. You
see, he has learned that there are
doors and windows in buildings,
and out of one of these a terrible
gun may bang at any time.
Though he has suspected that
Farmer Brown's boy would not
now try to harm him, Blacky is
naturally cautious and takes no

chances. So when he comes
spying around Farmer Brown's
house and barn, he does it when
he is quite sure that no one is
about, and he makes no noise
about it. First he sits in a tall
tree from which he can watch
Farmer Brown's home. When he
is quite sure that the way is
clear, he flies over to the Old
Orchard, and from there he in-
spects the barnyard, never once
making a sound. If he is quite
sure that no one is about, he
sometimes drops down into the
henyard and helps himself to
corn, if any happens to be there.

It was on one of these silent
visits that Blacky spied something
which he couldn't forget. It was

a box just inside the henhouse
door. In the box was some hay
and in that hay he was sure that
he had seen an egg. In fact, he
was sure that he saw two eggs
there. He might not have noticed
them but for the fact that a hen
had jumped down from that box,
making a terrible fuss. She
didn't seem frightened, but very
proud. What under the sun she
had to be proud about Blacky
couldn't understand, but he didn't
stay to find out. The noise she
was making made him nervous.
He was afraid that it would bring
some one to find out what was
going on. So he spread his black
wings and flew away as silently
as he had come.

As he was flying away he saw those eggs. You see, as he rose into the air, he managed to pass that open door in such a way that he could glance in. That one glance was enough You know Blacky's eyes are very sharp. He saw the hay in the box and the two eggs in the hay, and that was enough for him. From that instant Blacky the Crow began to scheme and plan to get one or both of those eggs. It seemed to him that he never, never, had wanted anything quite so much, and he was sure that he would not and could not be happy until he succeeded in getting one.

CHAPTER XXX

BLACKY SCREWS UP HIS COURAGE

IF out of sight, then out of mind. This is a saying which you often hear. It may be true sometimes, but it is very far from true at other times. Take the case of Blacky. He had had only a glance into that nest just inside the door of Farmer Brown's henhouse, but that glance had been enough to show him two eggs there. Then, as he flew away toward the Green Forest, those eggs were out of sight, of course. But do you think they were out of mind? Not much! No, indeed! In fact, those eggs

were very much in Blacky's mind.
He could n't think of anything else.
He flew straight to a certain tall
pine-tree in a lonely part of the
Green Forest. Whenever Blacky
wants to think or to plan mischief, he seeks that particular
tree, and in the shelter of its
broad branches he keeps out of
sight of curious eyes, and there
he sits as still as still can be.

"I want one of those eggs,"
muttered Blacky, as he settled
himself in comfort on a certain
particular spot on a certain particular branch of that tall pine-
tree. Indeed, that particular
branch might well be called the
"mischief branch," for on it
Blacky has thought out and

planned most of the mischief he
is so famous for. "Yes, sir,"
he continued, "I want one of
those eggs, and what is more, I
am going to have one."

He half closed his eyes and
tipped his head back and swal-
lowed a couple of times, as if he
already tasted one of those eggs.

"There is more in one of those
eggs than in a whole nestful of
Welcome Robin's eggs. It is a
very long time since I have been
lucky enough to taste a hen's
egg, and now is my chance. I
don't like having to go inside
that henhouse, even though it is
barely inside the door. I'm suspicious of doors. They have a
way of closing most unexpectedly.

I might see if I cannot get Unc'
Billy Possum to bring one of
those eggs out for me. But that
plan won't do, come to think of
it, because I can't trust Unc' Billy.
The old sinner is too fond of
eggs himself. I would be willing
to divide with him, but he would
be sure to eat his first, and I
fear that it would taste so good
that he would eat the other.
No. I 've got to get one of those
eggs myself. It is the only way
I can be sure of it.

"The thing to do is to make
sure that Farmer Brown's boy
and Farmer Brown himself are
nowhere about. They ought to
be down in the cornfield pretty
soon. With them down there, I

have only to watch my chance
and slip in. It won't take but
a second. Just a little courage,
Blacky, just a little courage!
Nothing in this world worth
having is gained without some
risk. The thing to do is to
make sure that the risk is as
small as possible."

Blacky shook out his feathers
and then flew out of the tall
pine-tree as silently as he had
flown into it. He headed straight
toward Farmer Brown's cornfield.
When he was near enough to see
all over the field, he dropped
down to the top of a fence post,
and there he waited. He didn't
have long to wait. In fact, he
had been there but a few minutes

when he spied two people coming down the Long Lane toward the cornfield. He looked at them sharply, and then gave a little sigh of satisfaction. They were Farmer Brown and Farmer Brown's boy. Presently they reached the cornfield and turned into it. Then they went to work, and Blacky knew that so far as they were concerned, the way was clear for him to visit the henyard.

He did n't fly straight there. Oh, my, no! Blacky is too clever to do anything like that. He flew toward the Green Forest. When he knew that he was out of sight of those in the cornfield, he turned and flew over to the

Old Orchard, and from the top of one of the old apple-trees he studied the henyard and the barnyard and Farmer Brown's house and the barn, to make absolutely sure that there was no danger near. When he was quite sure, he silently flew down into the henyard as he had done many times before. He pretended to be looking for scattered grains of corn, but all the time he was edging nearer and nearer to the open door of the henhouse. At last he could see the box with the hay in it. He walked right up to the open door and peered inside. There was nothing to be afraid of that he could see. Still he hesitated. He did hate to go

inside that door, even for a minute, and that is all it would take
to fly up to that nest and get
one of those eggs.

Blacky closed his eyes for just
a second, and when he did that
he seemed to see himself eating
one of those eggs. "What are
you afraid of?" he muttered to
himself as he opened his eyes.
Then with a hurried look in all
directions, he flew up to the edge
of the box. There lay the two
eggs!

CHAPTER XXXI

AN EGG THAT WOULDN'T BEHAVE

If you had an egg and it wouldn't behave
　　Just what would you do with that egg, may
　　　I ask?
To make an egg do what it don't want to do
　　Strikes me like a difficult sort of a task.

ALL of which is pure nonsense.
Of course. Who ever heard of an
egg either behaving or misbehaving?
Nobody. That is, nobody that I
know, unless it be Blacky. It is
best not to mention eggs in Blacky's
presence these days. They are a
forbidden topic when he is about.
Blacky is apt to be a little resent-
ful at the mere mention of an egg.
I don't know as I wholly blame

him. How would you feel if you *knew* you knew all there was to know about a thing, and then found out that you didn't know anything at all? Well, that is the way it is with Blacky the Crow.

If any one had told Blacky that he didn't know all there is to know about eggs, he would have laughed at the idea. Wasn't he, Blacky, hatched from an egg himself? And hadn't he, ever since he was big enough, hunted eggs and stolen eggs and eaten eggs? If he didn't know about eggs, who did? That is the way he would have talked before his visit to Farmer Brown's henhouse. It is since then that it has been unwise to mention eggs when Blacky is about.

When Blacky saw the two eggs
in the nest in Farmer Brown's henhouse how Blacky did wish that he
could take both.   But he could n't.
One would be all that he could
manage.   He must take his choice
and go away while the going was
good.   Which should he take?

It often happens in this life
that things which seem to be unimportant, mere trifles in themselves,
prove to be just the opposite.
Now, so far as Blacky could see,
it did n't make the least difference
which egg he took, excepting that
one was a little bigger than the
other.   As a matter of fact, it made
all the difference in the world.
One was brown and very good to
look at.   The other, the larger of

the two, was white and also very
good to look at. In fact, Blacky
thought it the better of the two
to look at, for it was very smooth
and shiny. So, partly on this
account, and partly because it was
the largest, Blacky chose the
white egg. He seized it in his
claws and started to fly with it,
but somehow he could not seem
to get a good grip on it. He
fluttered to the ground just outside
the door, and there he got a
better grip. Just as old Dandy-
cock the Rooster, with head down
and all the feathers on his neck
standing out with anger, came
charging at him, Blacky rose into
the air and started over the Old
Orchard toward the Green Forest.

Never had Blacky felt more like cawing at the top of his lungs. You see, he felt that he had been very smart, and I suspect that he also felt that he had been very brave. He would have liked to boast a little. But he didn't. He wisely held his tongue. It would be time enough to do his boasting after he had reached a place of safety and had eaten that egg.

He was halfway across the Old Orchard when he felt that egg beginning to slip. Now at best it isn't easy to carry an egg without breaking it. You know how very careful you have to be. Just imagine how Blacky felt when that egg began to slip. Do what he

STRIPED CHIPMUNK SAW SOMETHING WHITE
DROP FROM BLACKY'S CLAWS.

would, he could n't get a better grip
on it. It slipped a wee bit more.
Blacky started down towards the
ground. But he was n't quick
enough. Striped Chipmunk, watching Blacky from the old stone wall,
saw something white drop from
Blacky's claws. He saw Blacky
dash after it and clutch at it only
to miss it. Then the white thing
struck a branch of an old apple
tree, bounced off and fell to the
ground. Blacky followed it.

Striped Chipmunk stole very
softly through the grass to see
what Blacky was doing. Blacky
was standing close beside a white
thing that looked very much like
an egg. He was looking at it
with the queerest expression.

Now and then he would reach out and rap it sharply with his bill, and then look as if he did n't know what to make of it. He did n't. That egg was n't behaving right. It should have broken when it hit the branch of the apple tree. Certainly it should have broken when he struck it that way with his bill. However was he to eat that egg, if he could n't break the shell? Blacky did n't know.

CHAPTER XXXII

WHAT BLACKY DID WITH THE STOLEN EGG

BLACKY was puzzled. He didn't know what to make of that egg he had stolen from Farmer Brown's henhouse. It wasn't like any egg he ever had seen or even heard of. It was a beautiful-looking egg, and he had been sure that it would taste as good, quite as good as it looked. Even now he wasn't sure that if he could only taste it, it would be all that he had hoped. But how could he taste it, when he couldn't break that shell? He never had heard of such a shell. He doubted if anybody else ever

had, either. He had hammered at
it with his stout bill until he was
afraid that he would break that,
instead of the egg. The more he
tried to break into it and couldn't,
the hungrier he grew, and the more
certain that nothing else in all the
world could possibly taste so good.

But the Old Orchard was not
the place for him to work on that
egg. In the first place, it was too
near Farmer Brown's house. This
made Blacky uneasy. You see, he
had something of a guilty conscience. Not that he felt at all
a sense of having done wrong. To
his way of thinking, if he were
smart enough to get that egg, he
had just as much right to it as
any one else, particularly Farmer

Brown's boy. Yet he wasn't at all sure that Farmer Brown's boy would look at the matter quite that way. In fact, he had a feeling that Farmer Brown's boy would call him a thief if he should be discovered with that egg. Then, too, there were too many sharp eyes in the Old Orchard. He wanted to get away where he could be sure of being alone. Then if he couldn't break that shell, no one would be the wiser. So he picked up the egg and flew straight over to the Green Forest, and this time he managed to get there without dropping it.

Now you would never suspect Blacky the Crow, he of the sharp wits and crafty ways, of being

amused by bright things, would
you? But he is. In fact, Blacky
is quite like a little child in this
matter. Anything that is bright
and shiny interests Blacky right
away. If he finds anything of this
kind, he will take it away to a
certain secret place, and there he
will admire it and play with it
and finally hide it. If I did n't
know that it is n't so, because it
could n't possibly be so, I should
think that Blacky was some rela-
tion to certain small boys I know.
Always their pockets are filled with
all sorts of useless odds and ends
which they have picked up here
and there. Blacky has no pockets,
so he keeps his treasures of this
kind in a secret hiding-place, a

sort of treasure storehouse. He visits this secretly every day, uncovers his treasures, and gloats over them and plays with them, then carefully covers them up again.

First Blacky took this egg over near his home, and there he once more tried and tried and tried to break the shell. But the shell would n't break, not even when Blacky quite lost his temper and hammered at it for all he was worth. Then he gave the thing up as a bad matter and flew up to his favorite roost in the top of a tall pine-tree, leaving the egg on the ground. But from where he sat on his favorite roost in the tall pine-tree he could see that provoking egg, a little spot of

shining white. When a Jolly Little
Sunbeam found it and rested on
it, it was so very bright and shiny
that Blacky couldn't keep his eyes
off it.

Little by little he forgot that it
was an egg. At least, he forgot
that he wanted to eat it. He began
to find pleasure in just looking at
it. It might not satisfy his stomach,
but it certainly was very satisfying
to his eyes. He forgot to think of
it as a thing to eat, but began to
think of it wholly as a thing to look
at and admire. He was glad he
hadn't been able to break that shell.

Once more he spread his black
wings and flew down to the egg.
He cocked his head to one side
and looked at it. He cocked his

head to the other side and looked at it. He walked all around it, chuckling and saying to himself, "Pretty, pretty, pretty, pretty and all mine, mine, mine, mine! Pretty, pretty, and all mine!"

Than he craftily looked all about to make sure that no one was watching him. Having made quite sure, he rolled the egg over and turned it around and admired it to his heart's content. At last he picked it up and carried it to his treasure-house and covered it over very carefully. And there that china nest-egg, for that is what he had stolen, is still his chief treasure to this day, and Blacky still sometimes wonders what kind of a hen laid such a hard-shelled egg.

Blacky has had very many other adventures, but it would take another book to tell about all of them. That would be hardly fair to some of the other little people who also have had adventures and want them told to you. One of these is a beautiful little fellow who lives in the Green Forest, and so the next book will be Whitefoot the Wood Mouse.